The Theft of the Golden Torc

James Connell

Chapter One
The Theft of the Golden Torc

Awakened from the long somnolence of the night, the forest welcomed in the coming day with a chorus of bird song from high up in the tree canopy. Ground mist which had settled in the night before, had finally been dispersed by the rising sun. Dark shadows though, still lay in the dips and hollows, but they to in the end, had to give way to the pale pastel light of early morning.

From the high branches of a wild apple tree, a tiny figure emerged and stepped warily into the open. Dressed in a coarsely woven material which blended perfectly with his background, he was elfin in feature, and in size no bigger than the span of ones hand.

Throwing no more than a cursory glance to his surroundings, his attention focused towards the open woodland and forest stretching out before him. As "Keeper of the Watch," it was his responsibility to ensure that no danger emanated from this area of forest. Bringing into play his uncanny senses of sight and hearing, every part of the terrain was closely scrutinized, every noise detected and examined.

Not far away hidden by a deep gorge, the roar of the river heavy in spate from the previous nights rain, made itself known as it cascaded downhill towards the open sea. Close by, some small animals unwilling to be identified, scurried through the undergrowth leaving nothing more than a whisper of their passing.

As the warmth of the sun intensified, butterflies having dried their wings, took to the air spiralling and weaving in a choreography of dance and movement as they caught the warm currents swirling around them.

Not far away a male fox give a coughing bark to be answered almost immediately by its mate. As a final indication of normality, the bird song still emanating from the trees, was all the elf needed to quell any doubts he may have had. Satisfied he leapt down to one of the lower branches and making himself comfortable by wedging himself in a small fork of the tree, took out a miniature flute from his clothing and played to while away the time.

Against a background of swaying branches and rustling leaves, the music carried by the light breeze, waffled through the trees mesmerizing both creature and animal alike. Even the crows high-up in the tree line stopped their raucous squawking to listen to the surrealism of the flute. Engrossed in his playing he failed to notice ominous changes beginning to take place.

The animals who only moments before stood enthralled by his playing had quickly bolted and were gone. Oppressive in its nature and threatening with intensity, a brooding silence spread throughout the forest quelling all bird song.

The elf though had became oblivious to what was going on. The branches of the tree continued to sway with light momentum. Insects droned, stridulated and danced in the warmth of the sun.

By now he had lost all track of time and his eyes became heavy with sleep.

'I'll close them for a moment,' he murmured. 'just for a moment.'

Gradually the flute slipped from his hands, as his head drooped on to his chest.

Seconds later came the unmistakeable sound of snoring. The elf had fallen asleep.

Several hours later he was awakened by the loud barking of a dog. Jumping to his feet nearly cost him his life as he almost toppled over, with only his exceptional balance saving him.

The move though only antagonized a dog on the ground below. Baring white flashing teeth it took a tremendous leap upwards, almost reaching the lower branch where he was standing.

Quickly the elf willed himself to disappear, nothing happened. Puzzled he glanced down and to his horror, the gold ring which should have been on his index finger of his right hand was missing. Puzzlement turned instantly to fear. Without the ring his power was gone, and easy prey to all.

The dog, a black and white cross-bred collie was now sitting on its haunches watching every move he made. Realizing the danger, the elf grabbed his dagger.

'Think!' he whispered to himself. 'There must be a way to outsmart the beast.'

Suddenly his senses picked up a sound as yet some distance away but coming towards him. As he listened the expression on his face gradually changed as his worse fears were realized. It was a human voice calling to the dog.

The collie heard it as well which instantly drew attention to both of them with another frenzy of barking. By now the elf had recognized the voice as belonging to a child, but that made no difference to his predicament. Adult or child, all humans were alike when it came to getting their hands on fairy gold. They had an unquenchable thirst for it and would commit any barbaric act to possess it.

He gripped the dagger tightly. He would not be taken alive.

Within a few minutes a young twelve year old girl by the name of Jennifer, came into view. Unlike most girls of her age, she had none of her baby fat.

Athletic in appearance, with dark hair and a fair complexion, she was dressed in jeans with a boys shirt tied around her waist. Bold in manner, she looked every inch a tomboy.

Looking up she saw the dog and clambered uphill towards it. Grabbing it by its collar she admonished it with a shake of her finger. 'Towser! You naughty dog, running off like that…. Bad dog.' Next moment, she was hugging it tightly.

Although frightened, the elf was nevertheless astonished with the ease these human children were able to control these ferocious beasts.

Finally released from the girl's hold, the dog instantly ignored its mistress, and took another leap towards the lower branches of the tree with a frightening growl deep from within its throat.

Jennifer glanced up. 'What have you chased

up the tree then?'

Seeing the elf her eyes widened, and the mouth dropped open, For some time and was unable to speak. Disbelief and shock spread across her face.

Closing her eyes, she opened them hoping it was her imagination or that somehow, someone was playing a hoax. Throughout, the elf looked down with quiet calm.

Finally she found the voice to squeak. 'Are you for real?'

'Of course.'

To hear him speak only astounded her more. 'But who are you?'

Rising to his full height of six inches, he replied haughtily. 'I am kin to the Tuatha de Danaan and I am named after the great Cuchulainn himself.

Jennifer looked up in amazement. 'I don't understand.'

'Humans know the Tuatha de Danaan as fairies.'

Her eyes widened with excitement. 'Are you a fairy then?'

'No child. I am an elf.' We are kin. 'Are you going to harm me?'

'What on earth for?'

'Humans do.'

'Nonsense! I'm human and I certainly don't want to harm you.'

The conversation dried up after that which somehow developed into a strained silence between them as each weighed the other up. Fidgeting constantly and unable to control her patience, Jennifer finally asked. 'Can we not be friends?'

This could be one way of getting rid of the dog, he thought. 'Its unusual but

I don't see why not.'

'Good! That's settled then. By the way my name is Jennifer.'

'And as I have already told you, my name is Cuchulainn.'

The conversation petered again until Jennifer broke the silence again with an outburst of laughter. 'You looked so funny stuck up the tree. Can you not climb down?'

He was now in a quandary. Should he tell her the truth? He must return to his rath (fairy dwelling) immediately to warn his queen of impending danger.

He had to take the chance. 'I fell asleep Jennifer, and when I awoke I found that my ring was missing.'

'Was it valuable?' She asked politely.

You don't understand, the ring is the source of my power. Without it I am powerless.'

'Was that why you couldn't escape from my dog?'

He nodded. 'Can you control your beast? I must return to my rath.'

'Your what?'

'My home, its where I live.'

'Anything I can do?'

'Other than controlling that beast of yours, no.'

Her voice tinged with disappointment. 'Is that all?'

'Jennifer you do not understand. This is not a

game.   Even now, the little you know could endanger your life.'

'How are you going to get to whatever you call it without any help?'

Cuchulainn was extremely worried.   She was right of course. Yet the consequences to her could mean banishment or even death.

'If I were to permit you to go it could cause you extreme danger. Do you understand that?'

'Can you reach your home in time?'

Cuchulainn shook his head.

'Then I will help you.'

'In that case place me on your shoulder. I can direct you from there.'

Reaching up she grabbed Cuchulainn. He steadied himself by holding on to her hair. 'Lets go.'

'Wait a moment.'

Jennifer turned to the dog. 'Towser! Stay boy.'

Skulking back a few yards, it give a low whine before sitting down.

'He'll be all right till I return.'

Guided by her companion, Jennifer commenced the long climb uphill through the forest. Progress was often hampered by the long dense moor-land grass which tangled continually around her feet. The ground was very damp which made it difficult to keep a foothold. Brief moments of rest became more frequent as the climbed continued. Tricks of light and shade played havoc with her bearings, and in next to no time she was completely lost. 'Have we far to go?' she managed to gasp.

'No its just ahead. Come on, hurry.'

Forcing herself she staggered on until she came approached a small clearing.

'Stop here.' he ordered.

By now she was totally exhausted.

'Put me down.'

Kneeling she placed Cuchulainn upon ground and struggled back to her feet.

The clearing was nothing more than an open glade surrounded by a small copse of indigenous trees. Just off centre stood an old Hawthorn tree, weather-beaten and of indiscriminate age, encircled by a ring of boulders. Various small gifts such as beads, tinsel etc, together with bunches of withered flowers lay strewn, on and around the tree; anonymous gifts from human benefactors in the past.

There was nothing unusual in that, but what was, was the purplish-red berries clinging to the branches of the tree which were left untouched by the birds. The silence was finally broken by Cuchalainn in a tone low with intensity. 'Stay here and whatever happens, don't move or say anything. Your life depends on it.'

He walked between the boulders, stopped a few feet from the tree and spoke. 'I am Cuchulainn, Keeper of the Watch.'

With utter shock, Jennifer saw a tiny elfin figure whom she assumed was the Queen emerge openly on to a branch high up in the hawthorn tree. Several fairy attendants with delicate gossamer wings humming constantly, fussed around her continually. Dressed in a robe of white linen, she stepped off the branch and floated effortlessly to the ground. In moments, elf's and fairy alike poured out from the base of the tree to take up every available advantage point.

By now Jennifer had a closer look at the tiny queen and was amazed by her beauty. A flawless complexion, hair the colour of straw matched the startling blue of her eyes which were memorising in their look.

Giving Jennifer a momentarily look of haughty indifference, the queen dismissed her attendants then turned her attention to Cuchulainn.

'You have broken custom elf by bringing a human here. Explain yourself?'

'I had to your Majesty. Having lost my ring It was important to return as quickly as possible to warn you of possible danger.'

'How did you become to loose your ring?'

'He dropped is head embarrassed. 'I fell asleep your Majesty and when I awoke my ring was gone.'

'You fell asleep whilst on watch?' she asked incredulously.

In his dejection he failed to address her by title. 'Yes.' he whispered softly.

She turned on him. 'I am still your queen elf and you will address me as such.'

'I m sorry your Majesty.' he replied with a slight stutter.

Because of your negligence the Golden Torc has now been stolen. If it is not recovered by the rise of the moon on the morrow, this rath will perish.' And added softly. 'Dierdra will make sure of that.'

Miserably he dropped his head in shame. 'I am sorry your Majesty, do with me what you will.'

A shoot echoed from the background. No! .... Running forward, Jennifer scooped Cuchulainn up in her hands.

An angry roar resounded around the glade which the queen quelled immediately. floating upwards from the ground she landed on a branch which brought her eye to eye contact with Jennifer. 'I am Niamh, Queen of the Sidhe (fairies).... What business is it of yours human, if I should punish a foolish elf.

'He is my friend.' Jennifer replied simply.

'Your friend? don't be ridiculous. It is not custom for a human to befriend an elf.' She scrutinized Jennifer closely. 'Be honest with me child and no harm will come to you.'

'I only wanted to help Cuchulainn, that's all your Majesty.'

Realizing that she was telling the truth, the queen relented with a brief smile.

'What is your name child.?'

'Jennifer your Majesty.'

For a moment the name was misunderstood. 'Gwenevre?... That name was well known once for its tragic circumstances, but that was long ago.'

'Not Gwenevre your Majesty, but Jennifer.'

Swiftly her thoughts returned to the present. 'I'm sorry child. For one moment there I was thinking of someone else.'

'What is going to happen to Cuchulainn, your Majesty?'

'Jennifer your friend committed a very serious

offence and by custom, must be punished.'

'Whatever you had stolen, surely there must be some way of getting it back.?'

It was at this moment that Cuchulainn interrupted from the safety of her hand. 'No Jennifer,' he said sharply. 'doing what you did enabled me to return to my rath. Go home now, your parents will be worried.'

'No they wont. Anyhow my Ma and Da know where I am.' said Jennifer, fibbing blatantly.'

Niamh give Jennifer a thoughtful look. 'Do you mean what you say about helping this rath?'

'Of course I do.'

'Thoughtfully the queen looked at Jennifer. Now I find that strange. There is a prophecy among the Sidhe that one day a human will come to our aid.'

With some misgivings she continued. 'Surely it cannot be you, a child?'

'I don't see why not. I'm nearly thirteen.'

'I wonder.' Niamh was perplexed. After giving it some thought she came to a decision. 'What I am going to tell you could destroy this rath should it fall into the wrong hands.'

'I'm no blabber-mouth......'Your Majesty

A brief smile acknowledged the strange expression.

The seal of authority to rule this rath is the Golden Torc. As long as I have possession of the Torc, the tree above you will continue to blossom and bear fruit. Without the Torc, which has been stolen, it will loose its fruit and die.'

'And you your Majesty?'

'My power will be weakened to such an extent that I will be unable to oppose my sister.'

Jennifer glanced in amazement. 'Your sister? Is she behind all this?'

Niamh nodded briefly. 'My sister Dierdra, a sorceress of the Black Art follows Morrigan the Goddess of destruction and death. I am sure she had the Torc stolen, for by all accounts it has been taken to the castle of Dunluce overlooking the Great Sea. (Atlantic Ocean)

It is now protected by a Bean-Sidhe or Banshee as it is more commonly known by humans. So you see the danger you are letting yourself in for, should you attempt to help.'

'I'm not afraid of any old Banshee.' Jennifer replied with as much bravado as she could muster. Although the tone in her voice indicated otherwise. 'Anyhow no one would expect a human girl to try and get the Torc back.'

'That is correct child. Those who have sworn loyalty to my sister would not expect a mere child to make such a foolish quest.'

After a little thought the queen came to a decision. 'Take that elf from your hand and place him on your shoulder. I wish to speak to him.'

Jennifer did as she was told.

'You have a chance to redeem yourself elf, do you wish to take it?'

For the first time since the theft, Cuchulainn's face lit up. 'Of course your Majesty.'

'Then go and prepare. There is not much time.'

Jennifer placed Cuchulainn on the ground and

quickly he disappeared into a hole at the base of the tree.

'Your Majesty what does the Torc look like?'

'Shaped similar to a horseshoe it is made of gold worn around the neck as a sign of authority. Now before your friend returns we must do something with your height.   You are too conspicuous at the moment.'

'Will it hurt?' Jennifer asked somewhat timidly.

'Look at me child?' the queen ordered.

Jenny did so and in a moment she felt herself spinning around and around as if on a roundabout. A kaleidoscope of colours flashed before her eyes dazzling her into a daze. This went on for several seconds until gradually the spinning slowed down and finally stopped.   Coming to her senses she found herself lying on the ground.   Rising unsteadily to her feet, she suddenly realized that she had been reduced in size. 'Look at me!' she yelled gleefully.

The queen smiled.   'Now you will easily blend into the background.'

She was dressed in the same course material as when she first met Cu Chulainn.

'Its cool.'   Jennifer added excitedly.

At that moment Cu Chulainn returned and a look of surprise spread over Jennifer's face.   In place of the timid little elf she knew beforehand, now stood a miniature replica of a Celtic Warrior and armed to the teeth.

His clothing remained the same as it blended in with the forest.   It was the weapons which surprised her. A dagger and pouch sling was attached to a belt around the waist, whilst high across his right shoulder, the hilt of a sword peeped out from an elaborated scabbard of red corral.

Now that they were together, the queen gave them the facts. 'In the castle of Dunluce there is a large cavern embedded in its foundations which overlooks the Great Sea . Here in all possibility is where the Torc is hidden.'

Niamh's attention diverted to Jennifer. 'When I received word that the castle was being guarded by a Bean-Sidhe, I realized my sister must have had the Torc taken there.'

Jennifer was a little perplexed. 'You have mentioned the Banshee before, but what exactly is it.'

'The Bean-Sidhe is a Solitary fairy who has long been associated with death.

My sister now makes use of her for her own purposes. She has many disguises, the one most frequently associated with, is that of an old hag wrapped in a shawl. The one thing in your favour Jennifer is that she cannot cause you any physical harm.'

'What is there to be afraid of then?'

'Under no circumstances look into her eyes or you will loose your will for ever.

All she has to attack you with is her guile. Remember she has never matched herself against a human before who had prior knowledge of her strength.

'I'll be careful.'

'You still intend to go?'

'Of course.' showing more courage than she felt.

'So be it then.' Niamh nodded her head in acknowledgement. 'As for my sister, be wary of her although I do not think she will show herself in person.'

Jennifer was curious. 'Why is that?'

'She will not take the risk of using her magic directly in case something goes wrong. It would turn back on her.'

'That is why she uses the Banshee then?'

'That is so, but that is not to say that she is less dangerous.' Niamh's mood became more solemn. Jennifer have you ever heard of the "Children of Lir"?'

'No.'

'It's a sorrowful story. Long ago when myth and legend were fact, a great battle took place which saw the people of the Tuaths de Danaan defeated by a race of human warriors called the Milesians. Afterwards a new king was chosen. To try and keep the peace, the King offered his foster daughter in marriage to Lir. In time she bore him two sets of twins; the first a boy and a girl, the second two boys. She died shortly after and in due course Lir married her half sister.

After the wedding his second wife began to feel resentment that Lir should have loved someone else. In due course this resentment turned to hatred of both Lir and his children. One day she made the excuse of taking them to see their Grandfather, but stopped on the way and put a curse on them. They were turned into swans, but with the ability to speak.

Shocked the children wanted to know when they would be released form the curse, and were told only when a nobleman from the North married a noble-woman from the South, then they would they be released from the curse.

Nine hundred years passed before the curse was finally broken. By then it was too late. As they changed back into human form, they quickly withered up and died.

I tell you this Jennifer so that there is no doubt of what could happen to you.

I asked you before whether you wanted to go and you said yes .... After what you have now heard, do you still intend to go.'

Jennifer answered truthfully. 'I would be lying if I said I was not afraid.

She threw a glance at Cuchulainn. 'He will look after me if necessary.'

Niamh smiled approvingly. 'You are a brave girl Jennifer.'

'It is imperative that you return by the going down of the sun on the morrow or it will be too late. Be alert both of you.. All you have to protect yourselves are your instincts especially you Jennifer.' Giving her a direct look. 'The creatures you come up against will not have matched wits with a human before, so use your human ability wisely.'

She turned to Cu Chulainn. 'As for you elf, I believe that when you find the Torc you will retrieve your ring as well. Use your knowledge of the forest and the creatures who live in it. Make use of that and put your trust in nothing or no one other than yourselves.' The tiny queen became thoughtful.

'Your sole responsibility elf is to protect Jennifer at all times.' There was a change of tone. 'With your life if necessary.'

'I understand your Majesty.'

'Remember both of you, think before you act. Do not be wise after the event. By then it will be too late.'

The queen paused for a moment before continuing. 'The only help I can give you is to grant you one wish, should you need to use it. Other than that I can do no more. With the falling of the fruit, my strength is ebbing away.....

..... What I will do is this. In the forest, there is an old oak tree which is known to the elf. If you manage to reach it by the bewitching hour (evening), I will have three chariots there to escort you in.'

Niamh nodded to them both and disappeared into the base of the tree followed by the elf's and fairy's. In moments, the glade was back to its peaceful setting enjoying the warmth of the morning sun.

-o-o-o-o-o-o-o-

19

Chapter Two
The Quest

Now they were alone Jennifer took her time to examine her surroundings and became overwhelmed by the magnitude of it all. Her senses, especially that of smell and hearing intensified to such an extent that she could detect the faint aromatic scents thrown up by the Heathers and Honeysuckle from some distance away.

Everywhere she looked, she was surrounded by tall grasses, some coming up to her breast whilst others many times her size, threw off their seeds as they danced a graceful ballet of movement against a gentle breeze, which became almost hypnotic.

Yet within the beauty of it all, danger lurked to. Under the cover of the grasses, carnivores such as the fury hunting spider, bush cricket, scorpions and beetles especially the Soldier Beetle together with many others, waited their turn to pounce on the foolish or the unwary.

It was a sobering thought and it made her uncomfortable. She would have to learn the hazards of this new world she now found herself in very fast, or fall pry to the predator within.

'Chuchulainn I'm frightened, I don't think I am going to like this place.'

'It'll be all right Jennifer. It may seem strange to you now but you will soon get used to it..... I promise.'

'What happens now?'

'We go to Dunluce Castle?'

'How do we get there... fly?' she said sarcastically.

She was becoming her own self again.

'Cuchulainn laughed outright. 'As a matter of fact we do. Watch this.'

He put two fingers to his lips and whistled. Although undetected by Jennifer's senses as yet, within a few moments a herring gull swooped low over them and landed on a boulder. It give a wailing cry. 'Do you require my help?'

Jennifer give one incredible look of amazement. She could actually understand the gull.

'We need to go to Dunluce Castle?'

'Of course.'

Jennifer shook her head emphatically and looked hard at the bird. 'There is now way you are going to get me on that.'

Cuchulainn laughed outright. 'Its what you call cool.... Wait and see.'

Taking a leap on top the gull's back he made himself comfortable then held down his arm. 'Come? hold on to me if you want to.'

Taking a deep breath, she followed and landed behind Cuchulainn, and gripped him with a fierce hold around his waist. 'Could you not find something larger?'

'Dierdra has too many spies in the forest for us to use any of the creatures.

There is a reason for the gull. Its going to fly part way along the coast. If any predator should attempt to harm us, the gull will have the advantage over the open sea.

Closing her eyes, she gave a short whimper of complaint. 'Oh what have I let myself in for?'

Taking to the air, the gull circled the forest before heading of in an easterly direction. Realizing that she was not going to fall, she opened her eyes and looking down, saw the whole panorama of Glenariff Forest unfold below her with its contrasting versatility of woodland, forest and waterfalls wedged between two vertical cliffs rising up to two hundred feet in places, which ran parallel along a deep glacial valley of patchwork fields to the sea. Like the other eight glens, it was shaped during the ice age.

Fourteen miles away across a placid blue-green sea, the coastline of Scotland could be seen. Glenariff, often called the "Queen of the Glens" was a truly magnificent sight especially now as the forest had taken on its Autumn colours.

As the gull flew parallel to the coast Jennifer felt more at ease. Every now and again she would give a childish cry of delight and point to something which drew her attention, such as the glint of a tumbling river or a small picturesque cottage catching the morning sunlight.

'We'll be approaching Ballycastle shortly,' Cuchulainn shouted. 'from there we will fly inland to the Great Causeway (Giants Causeway) and then on to Dunluce. Have you enjoy the trip?'

Jennifer who was prone to fibbing answered. 'Of course I did and I wasn't frightened once .... Really.'

Leaving the coast, the gull cut inland and flew in a diagonal direction over a topography of moor-land, cultivated fields and forest. They were well into their flight now, and it still hadn't approached noon. They were ahead of tomorrow's schedule.

Jennifer was completely at ease now and managed to snuggle up against Cuchulainn's back and snatch some sleep. Some time later she was awakened.

'We must be near the coast again,' yelled Cuchulainn. 'I can smell the sea.'

Suddenly his attention was drawn to a speck in the sky above them. As he continued to observe, the unmistakeable outline of a peregrine falcon took shape.

'Danger gull.... Above you to your left.' He yelled a warning to Jennifer. 'A falcon above us. When it attacks, hold on to me tightly.'

'The flapping of wings and hovering of the falcon give every indication that it was going to attack. Suddenly the wings closed as it went into a controlled stoop diving on them at tremendous speed. Just before hitting its prey it levelled off slightly and slowed before trying to make, contact with the gull's wing.

Cuchulainn drew his sword and thrust it out to divert its attention long enough for it to miss.

With wings beating rapidly the falcon fought to gain height for another pass.

This time it made no mistake. Plunging down it diverted its attack at the last moment to the left side of the gull making it impossible for Cuchulainn to make use of his sword. The claws ripped savagely into the wing of its prey giving it a mortal wound.

In its excitement the young falcon dropped its prey, enabling the gull, to drop into a spiral. It righted itself close to the ground and more by instinct, made for its natural element, the open sea.

The fight had taken them of course, and with one wing badly blooded and beating feebly, the gull found itself just off shore being forced by the wind, towards a promontory of two hundred feet cliffs rising above them sharply.

Unfortunately in its weakened state it had not the strength to fight the wind, and was dropping rapidly towards a boulder strewn beach. It tried to gain height, but it was too weak. 'I'm sorry.' It screamed, and plunged. It was dead before it hit the ground.

Both fell heavily, and for a while were unconscious until Jennifer came to.

Clearing her head she clambered over to where Cuchulainn was lying a few yards away. She had great difficulty in climbing over the stones to reach him. 'Wake up! She shouted, shaking him roughly.

Moments later he awakened and rose unsteadily to his feet.

Jennifer was worried. 'Are you all right?'

'I will be in a moment.'

The beach was narrow and covered in pebbles and black basalt boulders The black precipitous cliff rising sheer above them was impossible to climb. By now Cuchulainn realized that he had lost his shield and sword in the fight.

Realizing the gravity of the situation, Jennifer spoke bluntly. 'We're trapped, the cliff's too steep to climb.'

From somewhere close by came the faint sound of whimpering from an animal in distress. Jennifer turned to find the source of the sound but

Cuchulainn interrupted. 'Leave it be Jennifer.'

Disconcerted by his cold indifference, Jennifer turned on him. 'Indeed I will not.'

'Jennifer death comes to us all. It is understood and accepted.

'That doesn't mean we have to stand by and do nothing. I'm going to help whatever it is.'

In her desperation to find the cause of the cry, she fell several times falling over slippery stones Finally searching the far side of the beach, she found a dog struggling to free itself from a wire trap. She yelled across to Cuchulainn.

'A dog's caught in a wire. Bring your dagger over and cut it free.'

Shaking his head he ran over and began hacking away at the thin copper wire just above a fishing hook which had embedded itself in the dogs collar. 'What is this?'

'Its what humans call a night line. They drive a stake into the sand and tie fishing line around it with hooks to catch the fish.' she explained. 'My Da told me all about it.'

Cu Chulainn shook his head in disgust. What a barbaric thing to do.'

Finally the dog was released . As it did so, a large wave rushed over them up the beach then subsided again.

'We cant stay here,' croaked the dog 'get on my back both of you.'

Clambering on to the dog, Jennifer and Cuchulainn held on tightly as another wave swept in. This time the dog let itself be swept into the open sea.

The currents which kept them close in-shore were too strong to fight. It was better to save energy until a suitable place to land could be found. Finally the dog saw the glint of sandy beach with cliffs towering above it. Nevertheless it was a chance worth to try. Slowly the dog swam slightly across, but with the current towards the shore. As they approached the beach, Cuchulainn could see a black basalt cliff bisected by a narrow ledge running diagonally up to the top.

Feeling wet sand under its paws the dog struggled a further couple of yards before it collapsed on to the beach, throwing its passengers off pretty hard.

Exhausted, all three lay where they fell.

Some time passed by before the dog showed the beginning of recovery.

Struggling to a standing position it gave itself a couple of shakes. Cuchulainn was the next to recover followed by Jennifer. 'She looked up at the dog towering high above her. 'You saved our lives dog, thank you.'

'And you mine missy.' barked the dog wagging its tail.

Cuchulainn interrupted. 'Are we far from Dunluce Castle?'

The dog barked a reply. 'Is that where your going?'

Getting no answer, it continued. 'Be careful, there is evil in the air. I can sense it.'

'Jennifer cut in. 'Can you take us there?'

'No! Cuchulainn said rather hastily.

'The dog can be trusted,' Jennifer argued. 'it has already save us once.'

'If you wish me to take you I will do so. My name is Ben by the way.'

It lay down to make it easier for them to climb on to its neck and grab its collar. Having settled themselves, the dog set off climbing up the narrow path which at times became dangerous due of loose gravel. Further up it had to contend with the hazards of a rockslide which collapsed part of the path sometime in the past, but in the end they reached the top in safety.

'If it hadn't been for you we would never have got this far.' said Jennifer.

Ben barked in acknowledgement.

Cuchulainn still wary of the dog, nevertheless acknowledged the sentiments.

'Have we far to go?'

'A few more miles yet.' the dog replied.

Rising to its feet again, the dog tested the ground for human scent.

Satisfied it lifted its head. 'We will go now. If we follow the path it will take us to what the humans call "Benbane Head." From there you should be withina short distance of the castle.'

The dog set off at a steady pace along a path which was often used by humans. It kept a steady look-out and when it had to, it darted into the undergrowth to let the humans pass by before joining up with the path again.

It was approaching late afternoon when the dog stopped on a barren part of the path. 'I will leave you here.' If I get too close, whatever is there may sense our coming.'

Cuchuainn addressed the dog for the first time by its name. 'In that case Ben, we will say our farewell to you with thanks and appreciation for the courage you have shown in getting us here.'

It give a low bark in reply. 'I must get home now or my master will become worried. You know what humans are like.'

The last remark was made to Jennifer.

'Lie down a moment Ben.' Jennifer asked.'

It did so with its face touching on the ground. She walked over and kissed it.

'I have a dog just like you back home. Thank you.'

With a wag of its tail it turned and disappeared back down the path it had come. They followed the contours of the coastline until they entered a farmers field with a wall running down the centre of it. A small stream ran alongside the wall which made the field completely sodden even in summer. Following some barbed wire fencing which ran along the cliff edge of the field to protect the cattle from falling over they came to the edge of the field overlooked by a deep gully.

Standing one hundred feet above ground on a promontory of basalt rock, with its grey weather-beaten ramparts, overlooking the sea, Dunluce Castle looked every bit for-boding as its reputation made it out to be. Surrounded by terrifying deep drops, the only access to it was by an arched bridge from the mainland.

Jennifer stood on tip-toe. 'I cant see the cavern?'

'Its facing the seaward side.'

'I've never seen a castle before.' she commented.

'This one you want to see only once.' came the grim reply.

'When are we going in?'

'Better wait until dark. By then any humans present will be gone.'

Jennifer noticed some rabbit holes close by along the banking. 'It might be a good idea to use one of those rabbit burrows to wait in until nightfall.'

'Your right. Once we're settled in, I'll go and try and find some food.

Examining a burrow entrance Jennifer found it dry, but what was it like inside? Then another thought occurred to her which made her approach Cuchulainn. 'You go in first and make sure there's no creepy crawlies.'

She shuddered. 'Just to be on the safe side.'

Cuchulainn disappeared inside and came out moments later. He smiled.

'Its clear.'

'Good, I hate creepy crawlies.'

She marched straight in followed by Cuchulainn and was pleasantly surprised. The place was dry and airy with other tunnels running off but they were now blocked up with earth.

As she sat back relaxed, Cuchulainn made

several trips returning each time with dry grass to make bedding. He also managed to bring some succulent berries with a few herbs including Comfrey, which were ate with relish.

'How long are we going to be here for?'

'Until darkness, why?'

'Why don't you tell me more about the fairies you live with?'

Now elves are great story tellers and Cuchulainn was no exception. 'I will.'

He paused a moment to gather his thoughts. 'A long time ago beyond myth and legend, a divine people ruled this land. They are known today as theTuatha-de Danann, or the people of the Goddess Danu. Magic and the supernatural were part of their every day lives and they lived close with nature.

During that time, several invaders tried to overcome Tuatha de Danaan but failed. Because of this invincibility they became arrogant enough to believe that they were immortal and therefore equal to the Gods themselves.

Unfortunately this arrogance was to be their downfall. There came a race who were mighty in battle and were known as the Milesians.

The first time they came, the Tuatha de Danaan won by the use of magic.

By now the Gods were angry with their arrogance. When the Milesians came again in greater numbers, the Tuatha de Danaan were forsaken.

Unable to use their magic the second time they were soundly beaten in a great battle and driven underground to live in the mounds and rath's left by an earlier race. In time they disappeared from the minds of men and because of their unimportance were forgotten. Yet despite all this, they were still able to interfere with affairs of humans. Do you want me to continue Jennifer?

Receiving no reply he glanced across and saw that she was fast asleep. Smiling to himself he made himself comfortable and nodded off.

It was the evening of the first day.

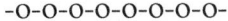

-o-o-o-o-o-o-o-o-

Chapter Three
The meeting of the Banshee

Late evening. Cuchulain awoke to the sound of a pigmy shrew foraging outside close to the burrow entrance for worms. They had overslept. Rising quickly to his feet, he crossed over to where Jennifer was lying and shook her gently. 'Jennifer its time to get up.'

'Oh Ma,' she replied sleepily. 'let me sleep.'

She was shaken harder. 'Jennifer wake up, its time to go.'

Opening her eyes she realized quickly where she was and hurried to her feet.

'I'm sorry. For a moment there I thought I was back home again.'

They ate the last of their food then went outside. Darkness had fallen but with the light of the moon Jennifer could see the outline of the castle very clearly. The complete eeriest of the place indicated that there were no humans about other than the headlights of a car as it passed by close by on the Portrush road close by.

Large black clouds scurrying across the sky, at times hid the face of the moon.

It was a perfect night for skulduggery.

Passing beneath a barbed wire fence they climbed down a steep incline on to a pebble beach. Treading carefully, they stumbled their way across to the side of the castle overlooking a lapping sea. They had to overcome large boulders now, and in doing so, finally arrived to the side of a great cavern and was confronted by a large opening, blacker than the darkest night.

Jennifer's first impression was that the darkness was just waiting to swallow them up. She give a shudder.

'Follow me and be on your guard.' Cuchulainn warned. 'If you see anything unusual, give a shout.'

'Don't worry, I will.'

'If the Torc is here, more than likely it will be hidden somewhere near the cavern ceiling.'

He took a deep breath. 'Right then, lets go.'

He scrambled round the boulders and entered into the sooty blackness of the cavern closely followed by Jennifer. Keeping close to the walls they traversed a narrow ledge and disappeared from view.

The only sound at the moment was the gentle lapping of the sea encroaching the floor of the cavern giving an indication of normality. There were ample hand holds, but the constant wetness of the walls made it precarious to climb.

This was making their ascent very slowly. Within a few minutes a ground mist appeared, sweeping in through the entrance.

'We have company.' Cuchulainn shouted.

'Where?'

'The mist. Keep climbing.'

Suddenly the mist began to swirl, rising upwards as it did so. Soon it took on the ethereal shape of an old hag dressed in a shawl who glared at them. 'Why are you climbing for, have you lost something? maybe I can help you my dears.'

'Look at me and tell me what your after?'

'Don't listen to her. Keep climbing.'

The Banshee took a closer look at Jennifer. 'A human child,' she screeched.

'What harm can I do you. Look at me and tell me so?'

'I wont. Go away.'

Quickly the crackling gave way to a low keening which was akin to an animal in distress. It was intended to distract them, but both ignored the apparition and kept on climbing.

Moments later Cuchulainn slipped on a wet foothold and fell on to a narrow ledge some way below. Jennifer noticed his predicament immediately as he was lying on a ledge staring upwards.

'Can you move?'

'No, my foot's caught.'

'I'm coming down. Keep your eyes closed.'

The Banshee saw an opportunity and took it. Floating upwards until she was hovering above Cuchulainn, and gazed down. 'You can open your eyes now.'

It was a perfect imitation of Jennifer's voice.

Cuchulainn opened his eyes.

'I've got you, screamed the Banshee.

Unable to move, Cuchulainn was unable to control himself from looking up. Her overwhelming power was too strong.

'Look at me! She screamed.

Jennifer leapt down beside him and lapped his face hard. 'Don't!' she ordered.

Shaking his head a few moments, he called out.

'I'm all right. Try and get my foot loose. Its wedged somewhere.'

The Banshee disappeared giving Jennifer the room to free his foot. Realizing he had a close call in giving in to the Banshee's will, Cuchulainn give a shiver.

'Come on, lets find the Torc and get out of here.'

Moving off together, Jennifer took the lead along a narrow outcrop which ran part way around the ceiling perimeter of the cavern. They were in total darkness now and everything had to be done by feel alone. Even Cuchulainn's uncanny senses were useless against the impregnable blackness.

After awhile of feeling every knack and cranny, Jennifer noticed something throwing off a glow in the darkness. She investigated it immediately.

'I may have found something.' she shouted.

'Be careful. It could be a trick.'

It wasn't though. Feeling her way she reached out her hand into a crevice and felt the Torc. 'I've got it.' she shouted.

'Good, pick it up and lets get out of here.'

'Keep it safe until we get outside.'

Jennifer put both articles away in her clothing, turned and followed Cuchulainn who began descending by a different route. Both were making good progress and without any further mishaps, had almost reached sea level when without warning, the ethereal glow of the Banshee appeared very quietly, her dark sombre eyes piercing them both with her stare.

The sudden quietness of her appearance startled

Cuchulainn to such an extent that as he glanced upwards, the Banshee transfixed him immediately with her gaze.

'I have you my beauty.' she screeched.

Jennifer a little way above him could not reach him in time and realized that he was beyond her help. Then she remembered the wish. 'Niamh queen of the fairies, I forgo my wish for your help in saving Cuchulainn.'

For what seemed an eternity nothing happened. Just as she was about to give up, a voice boomed out resounding around the black basalt walls. 'Who demands my help?'

'I do.' Jennifer said. 'My friend Cuchulainn has lost his will to the Banshee.'

Turning as she spoke, she saw the huge form of a Celtic Warrior appear.

Both he and the shield were engulfed in a shimmering light. The sword which he carried with his hand was raised ready to slash and thrust.

The Banshee met him with a laugh. 'Your too late warrior.' Rising up to his height, she continued. 'I have him now, he's mine.'

He attacked instantly with the sword but the thrust he made went straight through the apparition without causing any harm.

Jennifer give a scream as she saw what happened.

The Banshee give a crackle. 'Your weapons are useless against me warrior. Look at me and say so.'

'Don't!' yelled Jennifer.

'She was too late. Already the warrior was

beginning to lift his head.   All shecould do was to watch with horror.

'That's it now, look at me?'

Her whispered tone was as soothing as honey. Speaking, she raised her hands palms up and continued to mover them from the wrists, up and down, up and down willing him to life his head just a few inches more, and she would have him

Jennifer could do nothing but look knowing that all hope was gone.   As in a trance he was about to make eye contact with her, when at the very last moment he whipped up his shield.   Even in the darkness the ethereal glow from the shield reflected the Banshee's face back top her.

'No!..... Not me....'

A howl of fear went up from the old hag followed by a shrill keening which became weaker as the apparition began to evaporate.   Dispersing into mist again, it disappeared.   The Banshee was gone never to return.

The warrior examined Cuchulainn closely.

'Will he be all right?' Jennifer asked as she looked anxiously on.

The warrior smiled briefly.   'He wasn't under her spell long enough to cause any harm.   He'll waken up with a sore head.   Have you found the Torc?'

'Yes I have it in my pocket.   I also found Cuchulainn's ring.'

'That'll do him little good until Niamh restores its power.'

He glanced around for the last time.   'Its time to go.'

Picking up both of them with a scoop of his enormous hand, he carried them from the cavern, up the steep incline to a slip road running between a farmhouse and the castle, and on to the Portrush Road. He placed them both down very carefully. 'Little one your wish has been granted. I can do no more for you other than what I have done. From now on you have only your wits to relay on.

Be warned, by now Dierdia is already aware of the Banshee's demise. She will do everything to stop you from getting back with the Torc.'

'Why doesn't she finish us of now then?'

'Because of your little friend here. To wantonly kill an elf herself would be paramount to her own destruction. She will use her magic through sometime else or try and bring you both down. So beware.'

Jennifer's strength of character was beginning to shine through. 'I understand and I thank you warrior for saving my friend and also for your advice.'

At that moment Cuhulainn awakened and immediately held his head. He had in modern terms, what would be called a hangover.

Suddenly aware of the stranger in their midst, he lifted his head to follow his size and as he did so, toppled over and fell backwards.

Jennifer laughed outright which only made him madder.

Jumping to his feet Cuchulainn lifted up his hands in a boxer's stance. 'Did you push me there?'

'Don't be ridiculous,' Jennifer scolded. 'he has just saved your life. Put your fists down.'

There was a short pause before Jennifer asked somewhat worriedly. 'Do you remember anything at all?'

'Nothing.' came the surly reply.

'Is your head sore?'

'I'll get over it.' he replied gruffly.

The warrior interrupted the conversation. I will leave you now.'

'We don't even know your name warrior?' Jennifer stated.

The warrior replied with a grin. 'Ask your little friend here.'

'I never saw you before in my life.' muttered Cuchulainn, still nursing his sore head.

'You should.' The warrior shouted as he departed. Your named after me.'

Quickly he disappeared into the night.

Comprehension finally dawned. 'Stop!....
Wait!....' yelled Cuchulainn trying to run after him, but all he did was to fall down the banking on to the road. The warrior was gone. He was close to tears when he returned. 'My kinsman and I didn't even know.'

Jennifer was sympathetic. 'You didn't know. He'll understand.'

'Do you think so?'

'Of course he will.'

The wind blew in from the North bringing some sleet. Huddled together for warmth beneath a roadside bush, they waited for the shower to pass.

After some time the rain eased off. Jennifer

took the ring from her pocket and reached it to Cuchulainn hoping it would cheer him up. It worked. Upon seeing it his face lit up. 'Thank you Jennifer although its not much good at the moment.'

'I know. The warrior explained.'

An uneasy silence settle over them before Jennifer spoke again. 'I'm sorry Cuchulainn, but I had to forego my wish or the Banshee would have taken you.

'Its beginning to come back to me now.' A slight pause. 'That is twice you have saved me Jennifer from the Banshee. Thank you.'

'You would do the same for me.' she replied shyly.

Feeling embarrassed she changed the subject. 'We need to move, can we get help somewhere?'

'I'll see what I can do.'

This time her hearing was well attuned for she picked up the faint whistle as he put his fingers to his lips. They waited.

He seemed to have an affinity with all creatures for within a few moments, the cat-like face of a long-eared owl gave a small shriek like an oiled gate and landed close by.

Cuchulainn was surprised as he was not expecting an owl. 'Who are you?' he demanded.

'I've been sent by Niamh to warn you. Do not return by the coastal route.

Every creature under Dierdia's control are on the look-out for you. Find another way.'

Cuchulainn became suspicious. 'What direction has the queen advised?'

He had no intention of going where the owl suggested.

'None, but Niamh suggested to leave it to the human. She will find a way.'

'Without further adieu, the owl had taken wing and flew off.

Jennifer was perplexed. 'I don't see how I can. Anyhow why couldn't the owl have taken the Torc back?'

We accepted the task of retrieving the Torc. It would be against custom if we were to do otherwise.'

'What is this custom your always talking about?'

'It's the code we live by just like your human laws.'

The loud splatter of a vehicle's engine shattered the stillness of the night, as it wheezed and coughed to a stop. An open truck had broken down not far away.

'What's that?' Cuchulainn asked before he added disdainfully. 'Oh its only one of your human contraptions.' (Cuchulainn had a habit of calling anything a human made, a contraption.)

Jennifer laughed outright. 'I have an idea. That so called contraption is probably going to the market in Ballycastle. That is going to be our lift?'

'A what?'

'O never mine. Just follow me.'

Laughing again she climbed down the banking on to the slip road and followed it down to where it

41

joined the main road. The van with its bonnet up was parked by the side of the road, with the driver working on the engine.

Cuchulainn noticed Jennifer suddenly give a smile. 'What are you up to?'

'Hitching a ride to Ballycastle.'

Cuchulainn looked at her perplexed.

'Oh never mind,' Jennifer said laughing. 'Just follow me.'

Coming up to the rear of the truck, Jennifer noticed that the driver had parked it under an overhanging tree. 'We'll use the branches to drop into the truck. If the driver is going to market, we can get out there and make our way South. Maybe along the waywe can get help.'

Cuchulainn still looked doubtful. 'I've never been in one of these contraptions before.'

'Trust me, its cool.'

'That's what I'm afraid of.'

They climbed the banking and clinging perilously to one of the branches, they edged along it until they were over the truck's rear. Jennifer was the first to drop in followed by Cuchulainn who landed on a bag of potatoes with a loud

'Oh'.

'That hurt.... Now that we're in, how do we get out?'

'We'll think about that when the time comes.'

-o-o-o-o-o-o-oo--

Chapter Four
The Destruction of the Warren

Suddenly Cuchulainn give a cry of delight at the harvest of succulent fruit and vegetables lying in boxes all around him. 'At least we have enough to sustain us on our way.' he commented as he tucked into the fruit.

By now the problem with the engine had been solved. Closing the bonnet, the driver climbed into the van and drove off.

The distance from Dunluce Castle to the town of Ballycastle is approximately thirty three miles which they took advantage of in trying to snatch some sleep.

It was still night when the van reached the town. In just a few hours the same town would be bustling with shoppers. The vehicle stopped by an open stall and the driver stepped out to begin the task of unloading the fruit and vegetables

Jennifer awakened and in turn shook Cuchulainn. There was a some cord lying in the rear of van. She tied the end to a large bolt it and threw the rest over the tailboard. 'Come on Cuchulainn, we can climb up and over now.'

Seconds later they were both standing on firm ground. Keeping alert for stray dogs Jennifer took over and led the way clear of the market unto the beach, and then a narrow towpath running parallel to the river Gleneshesk, which they followed until a bridge blocked their way.

'Follow me.' she said abruptly.

Scrambling up the bank to a main road, she looked carefully for any signs of traffic before she signalled to Cuchulainn to cross, then followed swiftly herself.

Crossing the road safely, they found a way back down to the banking and followed it until they were clear of the town.

Gradually all signs of human habitation were left behind, but they were now in a quandary. With the coming daylight, it was impossible to stay on the path much longer in case of being seen by humans. To take to the open country, the tuff moor-land grasses would soon sap their strength and leave them helpless.

Having approached the perimeter of some woods they stopped to rest. The moon had hidden its face behind some cloud cover but even now the faint glow in the sky indicated that day was not far of.

Jennifer became worried at the lack of pace. 'We cant go on like this,' she said. 'we've got to take the chance and get help.'

Cuchulainn looked around him. 'I agree.'

Again he give another low whistle and waited. Some time passed before a buck rabbit hopped out from the undergrowth. Stopping, it stood on its hind legs and tested the breeze with its nose. Satisfied it dropped down again on all fours. 'One cannot be too careful. I heard your call.'

'We need your help to get to Glenariff Forest rabbit.' Jennifer stated.

'I know. All creatures have been warned to report you as soon as they see you. That is why I have been searching far away from my warren.' it explained calmly.

Cuchulainn examined the rabbit closely. 'Do you intend to report us?'

'No! … Dierdie is no friend of my warren. Anyhow we are too small and insignificant for her to take an interest in us. I will take you as far as Breen Wood. My name is Sorrel by the way and I belong to Hogweed's warren.

Climbing on to Sorrel's back they held on tightly as it give another sniff of the air before bounding off. With the warren some distance away, the buck set off at a blistering pace, but unknown to them they were already being watched from above. Two barn owls, loyal to Dierdie had witnessed the exchange and the rabbit giving help. Whilst one flew off to warn those ahead, the other owl remained behind to observe.

Knowing the route they were taking, an ambush was put into preparation by several foxes which was set by a small stream crossing. As Sorrel approached the area it sensed danger ahead. At this time of the year, ground mist is quite prevalent in this area especially before dawn. It made use of it now. It did not drop its pace though and made excellent progress. The low murmur of the river indicated it was close by. On their right, towering above them in the darkness rose the eighteen hundred feet peak of Knocklayd.

Now they reached the small stream to cross. One young fox being bloodied for its first kill, made the mistake of attacking early leaving a gap which Sorrel instantly took advantage of. Turning

45

nearly one hundred and eighty degrees, it jumped through the gap and away into some undergrowth growing close to the bank of the stream. It knew the area well, and just ahead of them was an entrance to an abandoned warren hidden by blackberry bushes.

Without stopping, Sorrel ran straight in. Jennifer was badly shaken by the experience, and as she jumped from Sorrel's back she was trembling uncontrollably.

Cuchulainn hurried to her immediately. 'Are you all right?'

'I will be. That was close.'

Sorrel interrupted. 'I'm going to find another exit. Wait here a moment.'

Somewhat later it returned. 'I think its safe now, we'll go. Both climbed back on and held on tightly to its loose neck fur. The main burrow being unblocked, they made good time as the tunnel was easy to negotiate. Coming out by the other exit, Sorrel looked out. 'Its clear.' It said.

It sped out of the burrow making immediately for the low ground where it could lose itself in the dips and hollows still covered in patches of ground mist.

Morning was approaching.

Sweeping low over the countryside, a curious young owl spotted Sorrel with his companions. Somewhat perturbed by the scene, it followed them.

Above, the older owl who had been tracking Sorrel saw the young owl, and believing it to have been sent by Naimh, prepared to attack.

Thus over the barren moor-land of the Antrim Plateau, during the darkened hours of early morning, the never ending story of life and death took place. The barn owl being older and wiser, swept low in a quiet glide as it approached its prey. Digging deeply with its talents into the young owls back, it killed it immediately, and carried it away in the darkness leaving only a few honey-coloured features spiralling to the ground.

They had now entered into Breen Wood and after awhile Sorrel stopped and stomped the ground. 'I'm letting my burrow know.'

At last they came to a field where in summer bluebells grew. A steep rise of banking covered by a hedge, ran parallel down one side to catch the early sun.

Sorrel approached a burrow and entered into one of the tunnels. Here the air was sweet, catching the scent of the heathers as a light breeze wafted through. At last they cane to a large space where several tunnels met. Here a very large buck was nibbling on a bunch of tender roots.

As Jennifer and Cuchulainn jumped of Sorrel's back it turned. 'I will leave you now.'

The large buck looked up. 'I see you have arrived safely. You will be provided for with a dry bed and some nourishment. My name is Hogweed and this is my warren.'

In accordance with custom, Cuhulainn give a slight bow. I thank you for your hospitality Hogweed, but we cannot stay. We must be on our way.

Jennifer stepped in. 'It would do us both good to take the offer Cuchulainn. We'll be fresher for the last leg of our journey.

Reluctantly Cuchulainn agreed. They were brought to a quiet part of a chamber where fruit and bedding had been left out. Within a few minutes they were fast asleep.

It seemed like no time they had their heads down when they were awakened by a young doe. 'It is time.'

They met Sorrel again outside the warren. 'I have volunteered to take you the next step of the way which is another warren close to your forest. Lets go.

Shortly after, Dierdie appeared by a copse of trees overlooking Hogweed's warren. Lifting her arms high she beseeched Morrigan. 'Goddess of the Black Art, my enemies have set against me. Give me the power to destroy all those who oppose me for by doing so, they have blatantly insulted you.'

Deidre knew that Jennifer and Cuchulainn had since left the warren, but she would destroy all those who give them shelter.

At first there was no sound, only a stillness, quiet and foreboding with the coming dawn. Then in the distance came twittering and squeaks clearly audible in the early air as a grey mass approached sweeping across the bluebell field.

Coming closer, the mass took form and were instantly recognized as rats. So many of them they could not be counted. Within minutes they were swirling around their mistress's feet. Deidre smiled and pointed to the warren. 'Go my children….. Kill!, Kill!'

The first to die were a few rabbits coming out to forage. With no time to warn the warren, they were killed instantly. More rats swarmed over the banking and entered the burrows taking those inside unawares. Inside the warren, the screaming began.

First came the cries of the weakest which were the summer's kittens, followed by the does and finally the bucks. Every cry heart rendering, every cry recognizable.

Along the perimeter of the field a young doe, given the name of Trefoil because of a small slash of yellow on her nose, had wandered off early to forage, and witnessed the whole thing. In fright she bounded away to try and catch up with Sorrel.

Within the warren itself, a few of the larger bucks including Hogweed managed to fight their way above ground, but the odds were too great. Yet they fought with courage and determination, and died where they stood. Only Hogweed was left but in the end its strength which was ebbing, was no match for the sheer numbers of rodents which overwhelmed it. It was a carnage of death.

Soon it was over and the rats retreated from view over a high rise, leaving behind the dead carcase's as a warning to all those who opposed Dierdie's will.

Ahead Sorrel was making good time. In the distance lay the towering peak of Slieveanorra and the forest to the left of it was where the warren lay. With a bit of luck, they should arrive with plenty

49

of time.

Morning had now dawned as Sorrel reached the perimeter of the warren. It again stamped the ground, notifying its arrival.

'Niamh will be told of your warren's help Sorrel,' said Cuchulainn. 'I promise you.'

Coming back down on all fours Sorrel raced the rest of the way and shortly all were enjoying the hospitality of another warren.

Having been given berries to eat they were escorted to a quiet area of the warren to rest awhile. Suddenly a commotion outside the side tunnel, caught their attention. Moments later two large bucks came into the tunnel.

'Come!' ordered a large buck menacing. 'At once or we will use force.'

Cuchulainn didn't argue. With Jennifer, they were both led outside of the burrow where several rabbits, including Trefoil and Sorrel, were waiting.

'What's wrong Sorrel?' Cuchulainn asked.

'Its Dierdie, she has destroyed the warren. Everyone's dead.'

'But how!.... What happened?' Jennifer cried.

'Trefoil here went out early to forage and saw the whole thing. Just after we left, Dierdie appeared with a plaque of rats and ordered them into the burrows. They killed everyone in the warren. The summer kittens, the does, the bucks... even Hogweed.....all gone.'

'Return with Trefoil, said Cuchulainn. it should be safe now. Give the warren a thorough check. If there are no survivors, start anew.'

'We will return at once.' Sorrel replied.

Without farewells, both turned and disappeared back into the woods. One of the bucks spoke. 'You cannot remain here any longer. You must go this instant or we will use force. We cannot help you.'

They were both escorted to the perimeter of the warren and given one last warning. 'For your own safety, do not return.'

The only option now was to walk, but with the full glare of daylight the danger became more acute. Within a short period they were totally exhausted.

Sitting down to rest momentarily, both fell asleep. By the time they awakened, the sun by now had dipped low in the sky.

There was panic in Cuchulainn's voice. 'We've overslept. We're not going to make it.'

'We've got to.' Jennifer replied.

He give another whistle, but no help came. 'The destruction of Hogweed's warren has spread across the forest. We'll get no help now.'

Hurrying on they were passing the remnants of an old cottage when Cuchulainn suddenly stopped causing Jennifer to bump up against him. 'Hidebehind those stones, we're being trailed.'

Trusting Cuchulainn instincts implicitly, Jennifer did as she was told. Awhile later a fox appeared nose down sniffing out their trail when Cuchulainn confronted it. 'Are you following us' he asked abruptly.

I caught scent of the human someway back. Those who are loyal to Dierdie have been warned of your coming. All known trails are covered so it is impossible to escape.'

'Why are you telling us this?'

'I was once loyal to Deidre but no more.'

Jennifer appeared from behind the rock. 'Why fox?'

There was a slight pause before it replied. 'Some time back I left my mate and cub whilst I went hunting. During the time I was away there was a slight altercation between my mate and two of Dierdie's foxes...'

For a moment it could not go on. Jennifer had to coach it. 'Go on.'

Humans say that animals don't cry, but when fox raised its head there were tears in those large dark greyish eyes. 'When I returned I found my cubs dead and my mate badly mauled. A short while later she to died from the wounds she received in defending the cub. Because of this I will help you.'

'No, wait! Cuchulainn warned.'

Jennifer was insistent. 'Its all right Cuchulainn, we're completely safe.'

Cuchulainn whispered in fox's ear, 'Play false fox, and I will kill you.'

'I will not fail you.'

It lay down on the ground. 'Climb on and hold tight.'

Moments later it was covering the ground at great pace. The speed filled

Jennifer with excitement. 'Run fox, run....'

Further on they passed another ruined cottage which was now just a mass of stones half buried in the ground covered with lichen and moss.

Nothing more than a testimony to those humans who came before.

The fox stopped suddenly.

'What's wrong fox.?'

'Get down both of you, we are being trailed.'

'Your right fox,' said Cuchulainn. the scent is too strong for one.'

'Can we outrun them?' Jennifer asked.

'No missy,' the fox replied. 'with two on our trail they would run us down no time.'

Jennifer was worried now. 'Is there any way we can slow them?'

It lay down. 'Go quickly. I will delay them.'

'Are you going to loose them? Jennifer asked innocently.

'Yes, something like that.'

Cuchulainn knew differently though. 'Fox when we first met I threatened to kill you...I am sorry.'

'Take the human and go.'

Sitting down on a small track, fox waited. It didn't take long.

When two foxes came round a bend of the path they were confronted by fox blocking their path. 'Stop!' It snarled.

'The one slightly ahead was the first to challenge with a short bark. 'Get out of our way, or Dierdie will hear about this.'

'No! the elf and the human are my friends.'

'Go away or we will do to you what we did to your cubs.'

Now many animals build themselves up for a confrontation. Some like big wild cats will snarl and roar before attacking, whilst others like the dog will growl and show teeth. Very few animals attack quietly. As soon as fox heard they were the culprits which the killed its cubs, it wasted no time and hurled itself silently at the leading fox catching it by the throat.

It took the second fox a little time to react. By then the first fox had fallen with its life blood seeping away into the ground.

Fox turned to meet the second adversary and both of them met head on.

Over and over the ground they rolled, snarling, kicking, biting. Fox managed again to grab the other by its throat but it to had suffered badly. Its right leg was almost severed, only held to the its body by the sinews. Blood was splattered all over it including its face.

In the end the other fox give the small whimper of a snarl, staggered a few paces, then collapsed and died.

Fox crawled to the safety of a hedge and fell. It tried to lick its wounds but by now it had been too feeble to do so. It lay panting for awhile, which became more shallow as it slipped into a coma. Moments later it died.

In time to come, the only witness to this tragedy would be the whitened bones to tell of the heroic deeds of a fox who give its life to save two friends.

At last Jennifer and Cuchulainn came in sight of the B14 which was the last barrier in their way, but time was against them by now. The late afternoon sun was almost gone and darkness was approaching. They still had two miles to travel to the old oak. Could they make it in time?

-o-o-o-o-o-o-o-o-o-

Chapter Four
Final Conflict

They were now on the outskirts of Glenariff Forest. Jennifer kept glancing back until finally she stopped. 'When is Fox going to join us?'

Knowing Jennifer by now, Cuhulainn found it hard to tell her the truth, but there was no other way. 'Fox wont be coming. To give us time to escape it sacrificed itself for us. We cannot waste the time it give us Jennifer. We've got to be moving on.

She didn't say anything as they hurried on, but there were tears in her eyes.

'Jennifer we have to take another chance as there is little time left.'

Suddenly a hare jumped out from the long grass.

'Stop!' Yelled Cuchulainn before it could bolt.

It turned and stood on its hind legs. 'I thought for a moment you were a fox. I smell its scent on you.'

Cuchulainn give it a thoughtful look. 'We need to get to the old oak. Is the path ahead clear?'

'All the forest trails are covered by Dierdie's imps.' The hare replied.

'Imps!...You've never mentioned them before Cuchulainn?' said Jenifer.

'Wait until you see them.' he replied grimly. He turned to the Hare. Is there any way we can make it to the old oak? He asked.

'If you wish I can take you.' Hare suggested.

'You could be putting yourself in danger.' Jennifer explained.

Unlike those rabbit vermin, I do not live in a hole in the ground, and I have no one to look after other than myself.' The hare explained.

Jennifer was shocked at the hare's cold-blooded opinion of rabbits.

'Climb on to my back.'

It tested the wind again before setting off through the long grass keeping to the natural contours of the land as it raced through the forest. The sun was almost down by the time it reached its destination.

Dropping both off, it turned and raced away without any farewells.

Now they had reached the old oak, were they too late? The tree itself was of an indiscriminate age. Creatures do not have long memories. All they will say is that long ago it was torn apart by a great storm. Yet it still nourished life.

Birds took shelter in its broken branches, and the wood itself was vibrant with insects and invertebrates like.

Cuchulainn was standing on the stump when he scrambled down, and put ear close to the ground. 'I can feel vibrations.'

Rising to his feet again he climbed back on one of the branches and waited.

A few moments later three fairy chariots, each pulled by two miniature horses broke out of the undergrowth and came to a racing stop in front of the tree.

Their horsemanship was truly superb.

'What kept you?' Cuchulauinn said with a smile. 'Late as usual.'

His three friends, Conor, Ossian and Donal leaped from their chariots and

After a few moments of bantering, Cuchulainn introduced his companion.

'By the way, this is Jennifer,' he said 'twice she has saved my life.'

Ossian gave a light bow. 'I thank you Jennifer, not though for saving my foolish friend Cuchulainn but for retrieving the Golden Torc.

Jennifer smiled. 'I take it that you are all elves?'

'The difference between our kin the fairies and ourselves are our height and elongated ears.' Ossian added with a laugh.

The salutations over it was now down to business.

'What are we up against?' Cuchulainn asked.

'A Cohort (100) of imps stand between us and the queen.' Conal replied calmly.

'And the queen?' Jennifer asked. 'Is she well.'

'As can be expected,' said Conor. 'Her power is almost gone now, so she cannot depend on her magic when the battle begins.

'So there will be a battle?' Cuchulainn enquired

'Oh yes. Conal added. Dierdie's army has formed and is about to attack.'

Conor chipped in. 'For by the destruction of Hogweed's warren, Dierdie has broken all custom by conjuring up these imps from the evil of the Black Abyss. If Dierdie is defeated, she will stand trial before the council at Tievebulliagh (The hill of the Fairies.) He threw Cuchulainn a glance. 'What do you intend to do.'

'Get Jennifer to queen Niamh as quick as possible.' said Cuchulainn.

He looked across to the nearest chariot. 'I'll take your chariot Donal. You go with Ossian and flank me on my left. You Conor on my right.'

'Remember, whatever happens, Jennifer must get through with the torc.'

'Before we go can we see the torc?' Donal asked Jennifer.

Jennifer looked at Cuchulainn who nodded briefly. She took it from her clothing and placed it in her hand briefly. It was the first time she had, had a good look at it.

The Golden Torc or Neck Ring was entwined with four strands of gold ending in two terminals parallel to each at the nape of the neck. Both ends of terminals were adorned with two boar's heads made of silver and had four blood red rubies inserted in the eye sockets. It was a beautiful piece of craftsmanship.

It was put away again quickly.

'Any questions? asked Cuchulainn.

A quick shake of heads give Cuchulainn his answer.

'Right then, lets mount.'

'Just a moment.' said Ossian.

He hurried over to his own chariot to return moments later with a spare sword complete scabbard harness. As you have a habit of loosing things, I thought you may need it.'

'Thank you my friend.' Cuchulainn said quietly.

Attaching the sword to his shoulder he climbed into the chariot followed by Jennifer. Turning, he reached her his dagger. 'To protect yourself if the need arises.'

Before taking the reins he checked over the case of the chariot. Light in weight and mobility it was made of ash, overlaid with weaved wicker. It heldseveral racks which were fully manned with spears and javelins. The case itself was roomy with enough space for one warrior, a driver and their equipment.

All drivers in this instance had been left behind.

Although the horses themselves were trained for the rein they were also trained for voice commands which was often used in the heat of battle.

A word of command and they set off at a trot in an arrow head formation.

The ground here was level and open which enabled them to cover it quickly.

Ahead though they could see imps forming up in line.

Closing in on their enemy, the fairy steeds on word command, changed into the gallop. With twenty feet to go, another command was given and the gallop turned into the charge, with all three chariots in unison with their distance.

Just before they hit the line, javelins and throwing spears were released directly ahead A break appeared in the line and the chariots swept through.

Jennifer had a look at the imps for the first time and shuddered. In size it was twice the size of an elf with arms reaching down below the knees. Their hands had long razor-like talents which they used to rake and disembowell when close in fighting.

The whole body was covered in hair especially around the face which was humanoid in appearance. On each side of the temples, just above a broad fore-head, grew two small horns but only on the male.

Their teeth were carnivorous which they brought into use when possible. From their rear protruded a short tail.

Clear of the first line the chariots continued their run.

In a few moments another line of imps were facing them. They made use of the last of their javelins as they fought their way through, but as they did so Donal lost his grip and fell from the casing. Surrounded by snarling imps he had little chance. The last Cuchulainn saw of his friend was the drawing of his sword followed by the roar of a Celtic war cry, echoing through the air.

'Farewell my friend.' He murmured.

'Conor was the next to go. They managed to kill the horses and pull him down. That was the last he was seen.

As Cuchulainn's chariot passed under some branches, two imps dropped into the chariot. As one grappled with Cuchulainn the other turned on Jennifer.

Closing her eyes she thrust forward with the dagger, and plunged it into its stomach. Screaming it fell from the chariot.

By now the other imp had raked Cuchulainn under the ribs which was bleeding profusely. Somehow he managed to throw it off far enough back to enable him to bring his sword into play. It died instantly.

'Are you all right?' shouted Jennifer.

He nodded but the pain on his face indicated otherwise.

Having now used up both throwing spears and javelin, they were unable to safeguard the horses.

Moments later they had to jump for it as the tiny stead's were mercilessly attacked and killed. All Ossian and Cuchulainn had now were their swords.

Not far away stood a very large chestnut tree. 'Make for the tree.'

Cuchulainn shouted. Fronting Jennifer with her back to the jutting roots, they made ready to make a last stand. The Celtic sword was a thrusting sword unlike the military sabre which has several uses. But here at close quarters, the fearsome sword came into its own.

Thus the two warriors fought. Rise, weld and thrust. Side by side they fought desperately protecting Jennifer as best they could. Cuchulainn stumbled and was raked again. Ossian jumped in front to protect his friend giving Jennifer the time to pull him back to his feet.

Moments later it was Ossian who fell. He was attacked from both sides and one of the imps disembowelled him. Dropping his sword, he clutched his stomach and with a loud 'Oh!' collapsed to his knees and fell face forward.

Bleeding profusely from several serious wounds, Cuchulainn turned to his companion. He touched her on the heart and kissed her gently as a human would do. 'Whatever happens, your one of us now human, farewell.'

Welding his sword with both hands he give a loud Celtic war cry. Protected by the tree roots they could only come at him one at a time whom he slaughtered with complete indifference. Suddenly in the background pandemonium raged.

The imps were being attacked by the birds of the forest. Crows, ravens and even the wood pigeons attacked, repeatedly going for the eyes, and in the dusk of evening, causing panic.

A bugle call bellowed, and from the undergrowth came foxes, mammals and the forest creatures loyal to Niamh with one thought in mind. Attack, attack, attack.

Once more the bugle sounded and from the undergrowth dozens of fairy chariots broke into the open, and where the fighting was fiercest, Niamh's highly coloured chariot could be clearly seen. 'To me elves … to me fairies… to me creatures of the forest… Attack!.. Attack!…Attack!

The combined force of fairy and creature alike, broke up the ranks of imps which left them exposed. In next to no time they were being badly mauled. As the battle raged there were no signs of Dierdie. She had disappeared. The imps on their own and without her help could not return to the Black Abyss. With no quarter given, they fought with savage desperation knowing they were facing death.

Naimh's chariot came to a running stop by Jennifer who by sheer strength, managed to kept Cuchulainn upright.

Jennifer was sobbing openly. 'He is loosing blood rapidly your Majesty.'

'He will be taken care of child.' She signalled and four elves carried Cuchulainn away.

'Can I go with him?'

'I'm afraid child that no humans may enter the "Other World."'

Jennifer took the Torc from her clothing and reached it over. 'Cuchulainn retrieved the Golden Torc she said straight-faced, and in doing so, has restored his good name in accordance with custom.'

'He will be acknowledged.' replied the queen.

Niamh held the torc high so that all could see and placed it around her neck to a tumultuous crescendo of sound. Having accepted the accolade which had been heartily, Niamh turned to Jennifer. 'You've saved this rath as it was foretold. In return for your help and courage, whatever you ask for is yours.'

By now Jennifer was unable to keep her eyes

open. 'All I want your Majesty is to go home.'

Niamh studied Jennifer closely. 'You are strange human. You have the opportunity of making yourself rich beyond your wildest dreams, yet you want nothing?'

Jennifer smiled tiredly. 'The only reason I did this was to help my friend Cuchulainn, your Majesty. He saved my life with the imps. His friendship is award enough.'

The queen thought for a moment. 'In that case accept this gift as a token of our thanks and respect.'

Niamh slipped a small gold ring on to the index finger of Jennifer's right hand. 'It comes with some power so be careful when you use it, and never let it out of your sight. Now to get you home. Close your eyes.?'

Jennifer did so and in moments she felt herself spinning around and around again. When she came to, she found herself lying on the ground by the wild apple tree withy the dog beside her.

Not fully conscious as soon as the dog saw movement, it started to bark then licked her face.

Within a few moments she was fully awake. She grabbed the dog and held on tightly. 'Oh Towser, I had such a wonderful dream.' She placed both hands on the ground to stand up and noticed a gold ring on the index finger of her right hand. She looked at it with complete shock.

'It wasn't a dream,' she murmured to herself. 'It actually happened.'

Giving a giggle, she called to Towser and ran down the hill with the dog barking furiously at her heels.

After awhile it became quiet again with the forest serene in a crisp September morning, bathed by the morning sun.

-o-o-o-o-o-o-

The End